By Constance Allen
Illustrated by David Prebenna

A Random House PICTUREBACK® Shape Book

CTW Books

Copyright © 1998 Children's Television Workshop (CTW). Sesame Street Muppets © 1998 The Jim Henson Company. All rights reserved under International and Pan-American Copyright Conventions. Published in the United States by Random House, Inc., New York, and simultaneously in Canada by Random House of Canada Limited, Toronto, in conjunction with Children's Television Workshop. Sesame Street, the Sesame Street sign, and CTW Books are trademarks and service marks of Children's Television Workshop. Originally published by Golden Books Publishing Company, Inc., in 1998. First Random House edition, 2000.

Library of Congress Catalog Card Number: 99-61341 ISBN: 0-375-80435-8

www.randomhouse.com/ctwbooks www.sesamestreet.com

Printed in the United States of America January 2000 10 9 8 7 6 5 4

PICTUREBACK and RANDOM HOUSE are registered trademarks of Random House, Inc.

Me want to cook a dinner.
Me need some help from you.
Let's send the invitations.
Then lots more stuff to do!

Please come to dinner.
We'll eat about eight.
Be sure to come hungry.
It's gonna taste great!
RSVP: COOKIE MONSTER

First we look at recipes,
Then we make a list.
Check it over carefully.
Anything we missed?

Next we shop for groceries.
Lots of things to buy.
Can't forget the pumpkin,
So we can bake a pie.

The house look kind of messy,
Let's make it nice and neat.
Then everything look better
When we sit down to eat.

Time to do the cooking.
Let's make the stuffing first.
Me like to chop up veggies,
But onions are the worst!

Next we baste the turkey.
Then we cook the peas.
Me like to put in pepper,
But it sometimes makes me sneeze!

ACHOOO!

Time to set the table.
Would you like to do it?
Should look just like this picture.
See? There's nothing to it!

Finally our friends are here!
Let's greet them with a smile.

But not polite to eat right now.
Supposed to chat a while.

At last it time for dinner!
All guests please take a seat.
Mmmmm! It tastes delicious,
Good enough to eat!

Time to wash the dishes.
Me give the soap a squirt.
After pots and pans all done,
We get to have dessert!

Now dessert's all eaten.
There's no more—take a look!
Tummy still feels hungry . . .